W9-AVO-908

SADDLEBACK
PUBLISHING·INC.

Barclay
Family
Adventures
SERIES
2

Mystery at Bear Lake

BY

Ed Hanson

THE BARCLAY FAMILY ADVENTURES

Series 1	Series 2
Amazon Adventure	African Safari
Danger at 20 Fathoms	Disaster in Oceania
Desert Ordeal	Falsely Accused
Forest Fire	The Floodgates
Hostages	Free Fall
Lost at Sea	Hurricane
Mountain Blizzard	Iron Mountain
The Pass	**Mystery at Bear Lake**
The Swamp	Ransom
Tornado	Sunken Treasure

Development and Production: Laurel Associates, Inc.
Cover and Interior Art: Black Eagle Productions

SADDLEBACK
PUBLISHING·INC.
Three Watson
Irvine, CA 92618-2767
Website: www.sdlback.com

ISBN 1-56254-807-7

Printed in the United States of America
10 09 08 07 06 05   9 8 7 6 5 4 3 2 1

CONTENTS

MEET THE BARCLAYS

Paul Barclay
A fun-loving father of three who includes his kids in his adventures whenever he can.

Ann Barclay
The devoted mother who manages the homefront during Paul's many absences as an on-site construction engineer.

Jim Barclay
The eldest child, Jim is a talented athlete in his third year of college on a football scholarship.

Aaron Barclay
A high school senior, Aaron is inquisitive, daring, and an absolute whiz in science class.

Pam Barclay
Adopted from Korea as a baby, Pam is a spunky high school freshman who more than holds her own with her lively older brothers.

The Mystery Begins

Scoutmaster Chuck Bates whistled as he stirred the stew that was bubbling on the propane camp stove. He was a happy man, doing what he loved best. What could be more fun than taking a group of scouts on a nature weekend in the mountains?

They'd hiked for seven hours to get to the campsite. Now they were on the edge of Bear Lake, miles from civilization. Chuck had assigned one or two specific tasks to each member of the small group. The large tent had to be assembled. Wood for the campfire had to be gathered. And someone had to chop up the vegetables for the scoutmaster's famous stew.

Finally, they'd finished all their chores. Now they were free to sit around the campfire and enjoy the delicious meal. Charlie Wilson, a boy whose nickname was "Red," spoke up. "Why is it that food always seems to taste better outdoors?" he wondered aloud.

A boy named Steve Jackson laughed. "Maybe it's because we hiked for seven hours today," he said. "By the time dinner was ready we were all starving."

Mr. Bates smiled. "No, no!" he said. "The real reason it tastes so good is because I'm such a fine cook."

The boys continued to banter for another hour. Then Chuck Bates suggested that they clean up the dishes. After finishing that chore the scouts sat around the fire. They swapped horror stories for a couple of hours. Before turning in for the night, they voted on who had told the scariest tale. Paul Riggs won. His tale was about a human hand that somehow took on a life of its own and went on a killing spree.

Seven scouts, spread out in sleeping bags, crowded the big tent. After their long day, sleep came easily.

It was about 2:00 A.M. when Charlie Wilson awoke with the need to go to the bathroom. The thought of trudging out in the cool night air wasn't very appealing. Charlie tried to go back to sleep, but couldn't. So he climbed out of his sleeping bag, grabbed his flashlight, and headed out into the night.

Charlie was about 20 yards from the tent when something struck him from behind. The terrific force of the blow drove him to the ground. Charlie was stunned. He tried to scream, but his face was buried in leaves on the forest floor. Whatever had attacked him was obviously very big and extremely strong.

Charlie Wilson struggled, but it was

hopeless. The last thing he remembered was being dragged from the tent site and carried deep into the forest.

At 6:30 A.M., the sun was just peeking over the lake. The scouts sleeping in the tent started to stretch and stir.

"Rise and shine!" Mr. Bates shouted.

Paul Newton, who was nicknamed "Fig," looked at his watch. "It's only 6:30," he grumbled. "Can't we sleep for just one more hour?"

Mr. Bates smiled. "Just for that, Fig, you can peel the potatoes for the pan fries," he replied cheerfully.

One of the boys looked around the tent. "Hey, where's Red?" he asked.

"I'll bet he's down at the lake, probably having a swim," Paul Riggs suggested.

Ten minutes later they all piled out of the tent. Not finding Charlie at the lake, they started calling out to him. When they still got no answer, Scoutmaster Bates started to worry.

"Okay, guys, let's spread out in all directions and look around. He can't have gone very far."

Minutes later Fig Newton called out, "Over here! I found his flashlight."

Chuck Bates studied the ground around the flashlight. The disturbed leaves seemed to indicate that some kind of struggle had gone on there. But something else frightened him even more. Some of the leaves appeared to have been splashed with blood!

Scoutmaster Bates roped off the area. He told the boys to stay away so they wouldn't disturb any other clues. Hurrying back to the tent, he got out his cell phone. His first call was to the local police department. His second was to the forestry service.

About two hours later a helicopter landed on the lakeshore. Personnel from both departments were aboard.

The officers went over the roped-off

area with a fine-toothed comb. Other than the flashlight and the few bloody leaves, no more clues were found. They tried to find a trail leading away from the lake. But with so many leaves on the ground it was impossible to identify any tracks.

More police officers and forestry officials rushed to the campsite. They examined the area for two full days. But in spite of their efforts, they found nothing. Someone—or something—had apparently made off with Charlie "Red" Wilson. And no one had the slightest idea who—or *what*—could have done such a thing.

A Gruesome Discovery

Two weeks had passed since the disappearance of Charlie Wilson. The authorities were baffled. They'd ruled out a black bear attack. That animal was the major large predator in the Northeast. Officials knew that black bear attacks on humans were rare. And when an attack occurs, the body is always mauled where it falls. No, this was something different. Everyone was sure of that.

The following day the phone rang at the Rockdale Police Department. Since Sergeant Peters was on desk duty, he took the call.

"This is Paula Cutts," a woman said.

Her voice was shaking. "I want to report that my husband Sam is missing."

"How long has he been gone?" asked Sergeant Peters.

"Since yesterday," she replied. "He went fly fishing at Bear Lake and hasn't returned."

Sgt. Peters tried to reassure her. "That's a long hike to get up there, Mrs. Cutts. Perhaps he decided to stay the night."

"No, he wouldn't do that!" she cried out. "And he didn't hike in. He has an all-terrain vehicle, so his drive to the lake would take less than an hour."

"Let me talk to my chief about this," Peters said. "I'll call you back right away." After writing down her telephone number, he hurried down the hallway to Chief Bell's office.

Roy Bell had been chief of police in Rockdale for the past six years. He was respected by the townspeople and well-liked by his officers. He looked up when

Peters walked into his office. "We just got notice of a missing person, Chief," Peters reported.

"Oh?" Chief Bell replied.

"Yes, sir," Peters continued. "A woman called to say that her husband went fishing up at Bear Lake and never returned."

The mention of Bear Lake got Chief Bell's immediate attention. Two weeks earlier he'd been up there looking for a missing Boy Scout.

"Okay, just give me the information, Sergeant," Chief Bell said. "I'll take it from here."

Once informed, Chief Bell quickly got on the phone to Tim Ward, the head of the forest service. "Chief Roy Bell here," he said crisply. "Does the name 'Bear Lake' ring a bell with you, Tim?"

"It sure does," Ward responded. "That's where that Boy Scout disappeared two weeks ago, isn't it, Roy?"

"Exactly," Bell said. "Now I've had a

call from a woman who claims that her husband is missing. She says he never returned from a fishing trip up there. I'm going out to talk with her. It occurred to me that you might want to come along."

"Yes, Chief, I definitely would," Ward answered. "I can be at your office in 20 minutes."

Half an hour later the two men were driving to Paula Cutts's house. Frowning, Roy turned to Tim. "For some reason I have a very bad feeling about this."

"That's strange—so do I," Tim said. "In fact, I've been feeling uneasy about Bear Lake ever since that Boy Scout went missing."

After talking with Mrs. Cutts, Chief Bell organized a search party. It was already too late in the day to get started. So Tim and Roy agreed to head out at first light. Several friends of the Cutts family volunteered to go along.

The nine-member search party reached

Bear Lake just before 8:00 A.M. The first thing they saw was Sam Cutts's ATV parked by the edge of the lake.

Roy divided the volunteers into two groups so the shoreline could be searched in both directions at once. "We'll meet back here at 10:00 A.M.," he told them.

Hiking around the lake was difficult. In places the thick forest extended right to the water's edge. By spreading out, Roy's group covered a large area around the edge of the lake. An hour and a half later, they'd found nothing. Chief Bell suggested that they rendezvous with the other group.

As Roy approached the meeting area, he could see that the second group had already arrived. He sensed sadness on their faces and feared the worst.

As he got closer, he called out to Tim. "I'm sorry to say that we found nothing. How did you folks do?"

Tim Ward said nothing, but his face was grim. As Roy walked up to him, Tim slowly unfolded the tattered remains of a bloodstained shirt. Inside the shirt lay a *human hand!*

Roy stared in shock at the gruesome discovery. As this hand had been ripped from the victim's arm, its wrist bones had been crushed. He opened his mouth, but couldn't speak. Sensing Roy's question, Tim said, "Cutts was attacked about a quarter mile from here. There's a fair amount of blood at the scene—but no sign of the rest of the body."

"Chief Bell," one of the searchers spoke up, "we searched for a half-mile in every direction. Whatever or whoever did this seems to have vanished."

Roy sighed. "We should all get back to town now," he said. "And if we come up here again, let's make sure that we're heavily armed."

The First Clue

Just as the search party arrived at Bear Lake, Pam Barclay was preparing for her morning run. As a first-year track athlete, she'd done well in the shorter races. Now the coach wanted her to train for the cross-country team. That meant her practice runs were longer. Today's 10-mile run would take her along a wooded trail just a few miles south of Bear Lake.

Pam's good friend and teammate, Marci Palmer, would join her on the run. For a while the two girls jogged along effortlessly, talking and laughing as they ran. Their routine was always the same. For the first eight miles they'd stay together. Then, with two miles left to go, the girls would pick up the pace. Each would attempt to be first at the finish line. As Pam was a faster sprinter, she usually won by 100 yards or more.

At the seven-mile mark, the girls were deep in the forest—just a few miles from Bear Lake. As they jogged along, neither one was aware of the large creature running with them. It was just 25 yards off the path. Silently and effortlessly it kept pace with the two girls—even though it was running through underbrush and heavy stands of trees. Its red, bloodshot eyes glared with menace at these intruders to the forest.

At last the girls approached the big, white boulder that marked eight miles. Pam shouted, "I'll see you at the finish!" and started to pull away. Her pace was very fast. Marci was afraid of tiring in the last half-mile. So she settled into a slower pace and watched Pam disappear down the trail.

Pam was about 40 yards ahead when she thought she heard a scream. She

stopped and listened. There it was again—
a truly horrifying shriek. It seemed to
come from behind—near the eight-mile
mark. With no thought for her own safety,
Pam ran back up the trail.

She rounded a bend just in time to see
something disappearing into the woods.
Now Pam started screaming as loud as she
could. At the same time, she picked up a
large branch. As she neared the spot where
the creature had left the trail, she banged
the branch on the ground. It worked!
Whatever it was had dropped Marci's body
and run off into the forest.

Pam's heart was thumping in her chest
as she approached the fallen girl. "Marci,
are you all right?" she whispered.

Marci didn't respond. She just gazed at
her friend in shock. Blood was streaming
down her face from a cut on her forehead.
Her left arm was also bleeding badly. To
stem the flow, Pam took off her headband
and tied it around Marci's arm. Then she
hoisted her friend onto her back and

started to carry her down the trail, piggyback style. "Don't worry, Marci," she murmured. "I'll get you out of here."

Normally, Pam could have run the last two miles in 14 or 15 minutes. But struggling down the trail with Marci on her back took nearly an hour. When she reached the main road she flagged the first car that came by. A half-hour later Marci was being treated at the hospital.

In the waiting room, Pam called Marci's mother first. Then she called her father and told him about the attack. Both assured Pam they would be right there.

Just before leaving, Paul placed a call to Chief Roy Bell at the police station. The Chief was stunned. He'd just gotten back from Bear Lake himself. The grisly image of the mutilated hand was still very fresh in his mind.

"Paul, I've got to talk with your daughter," Chief Bell said urgently. "I'll meet you at the hospital." He hung up before Paul had time to reply.

Both men arrived at the hospital at the same time. "Hello, Roy," Paul said as he shook the Chief's hand. "Thanks for making the trip, but I could have brought Pam by your office."

Roy sighed. "Yeah, I know you could have, Paul. But something *very* strange is happening in the woods around Bear Lake," he said worriedly. "You probably read about that Boy Scout who went missing a few weeks ago. Now a fisherman is missing, too. And from what we found at the lake earlier today, he's not going to be found alive. I'm just hoping that Pam saw something that can help us," he concluded.

As they walked into the waiting room, Pam was talking with one of the doctors. "There you are! This is my father and Chief Bell," she said to the doctor.

The doctor turned to Paul. "You should be very proud of this young woman, Mr. Barclay," he said. "There's no doubt that she saved her friend's life. The tourniquet she tied around the girl's arm effectively stopped the bleeding. And I understand she then carried her down the mountain."

Pam's face flooded with relief. "Then you think Marci's going to be okay?" she asked hopefully.

"Yes, I think so," the doctor replied. "She might have some minor scarring on her forehead and arm, but that's about it."

"Oh, thank God!" a woman's voice cried out.

They all turned to see Marci's mother rushing up behind them. Tears were streaming down her face.

Mrs. Palmer threw her arms around Pam. "I am forever grateful to you," she said sincerely.

Then Marci's mother turned to face the doctor. "Can I see my daughter now?" she asked.

"Yes, of course," the doctor replied. "She's sleeping now. But I'm sure it will do her a world of good to see her mother's face when she wakes up."

As Mrs. Palmer and the doctor walked off, Chief Bell turned to Pam. "I need to ask you a few questions," he said.

"Yes, sir," Pam replied.

Chief Bell looked intently at Pam. "What *exactly* did you see?" he asked. "Can you describe who or what attacked Marci?"

"Gosh, Chief, everything happened so fast that it's all sort of a blur," Pam replied. "When I heard Marci scream, I came running. As I rounded the bend, I got just a brief glimpse of whatever it was."

"Think hard, Pam," the Chief prodded. "You said 'what'—not 'who.' Why is that?"

Pam closed her eyes for a few seconds. "Well," she finally responded, "the creature I saw was walking on all fours—and it had a long tail!"

An Explanation

For the time being the authorities were trying to keep the attacks a secret. Chief Bell was concerned about panicking local residents. He was also fearful that hunters from miles away would rush up to Bear Lake with their rifles. But it was too late now. The headline in the local paper read:

MYSTERIOUS CREATURE ATTACKS THIRD VICTIM

As the only person who'd seen the beast, Pam Barclay had become something of a celebrity. Her parents did their best to protect her from reporters. After all, she'd seen very little—and she'd already reported that to the police.

Late the next afternoon Roy Bell received a phone call. "Chief Bell? This is

Professor Markum," a deep voice said. "I was a research biologist with the Higgins Institute—until it was destroyed by that tornado two years ago."

"Oh, yes," Chief Bell said. "I remember the Institute and the storm, too. It leveled most of your buildings, as I recall."

"That's right, sir, it did," Markum replied. "The damage was so severe that we decided not to rebuild. I'm calling now to tell you about a situation that may have a bearing on your, uh—problem up at Bear Lake."

"Go on," Chief Bell urged.

"I'd rather not discuss this matter on the telephone, Chief," Markum said. "But I can be in your office tomorrow morning. How does 9:00 A.M. sound?"

"That's fine," the Chief agreed. "I'll probably invite a few other people who'll be interested in what you have to say."

Tim Ward and Paul Barclay should sit in on this meeting, he thought.

It was shortly after 9:00 A.M. when the professor walked into the station. He was a tall, slender man with thick glasses and graying hair. Paul whispered to Roy, "He sure looks like a scientist, doesn't he?"

After introductions were made, the four men took seats at the table. Markum was the first to speak. "Four years ago the Higgins Institute took on a most ambitious project. Our goal was to protect an endangered species—and perhaps, in the process, create a new life form." The room was silent as the professor went on.

"You probably realize that the tiger is on the verge of extinction all over our planet. That's why we decided to create a hybrid by using the tiger's genetic material. We set out to fertilize the egg of a mountain lion with the sperm of a Siberian tiger. The experiments were conducted in our laboratory."

Roy, Tim, and Paul glanced at each other nervously. Each was too stunned to speak. "I was put in charge of the project," Markum continued. "My specialty is molecular biology, you see. We purchased the eggs and the sperm from different zoos around the country. For more than a year we worked without success. Then about three years ago a miracle happened. We had a fertilized egg! After inserting it into a healthy female cougar, the waiting began.

"Four months later the cougar gave birth to a male cub. It was a cross between our mountain lion and a tiger. As you can imagine, the scientific significance of this accomplishment is breathtaking! The cub grew rapidly. In just four months it out-weighed its mother by 50 pounds.

"When the tornado struck, we were just getting ready to make our announcement to the world." He sighed deeply before going on. "As you know, the Institute was totally destroyed. We found the mother's body buried under some rubble. We could only assume that the cub had been killed as well. But now that we hear about what's been happening at Bear Lake, I'm not so sure."

"If your creation is still alive, how large would it be by now?" Tim Ward asked. "And why would it be attacking humans?"

"Those are good questions, but I can only guess at the answers," Markum replied. "The tiger is the largest cat in the world. An adult male can reach about 500 pounds. That makes it considerably larger than the African lion. My guess is that it's now about 300 to 350 pounds."

Chief Bell glared at Markum. "How could you have just *assumed* the cub was dead when you couldn't find the body?" he said angrily. "At the very least, you should have advised the authorities of the situation."

"You're absolutely right," Markum replied. "It was a mistake on our part, and we're terribly sorry. I only hope we can redeem ourselves now, because there's something else—"

"And *that* would be?" the Chief asked.

"Well, deer would be the usual prey for a tiger in these parts," Markum went on.

"And there are certainly plenty of deer in the woods around Bear Lake. But if our cat was ill or injured, it might become difficult for it to catch deer. In that case, *humans* would be an easier prey."

Tim Ward spoke up next. "I have only one response to that: How do we kill this creation of yours before it takes another human life?"

"Sir, you can't be *serious!*" Markum yelped in outrage. "An exciting new life form has been created. If we can get it to reproduce, future generations will be all the richer. *Of course* we don't want it attacking people. But killing it isn't the answer! We have to capture it so it can be cared for in a zoo or a wildlife preserve."

Paul had remained thoughtfully silent, but now he spoke up. "And how do you suggest we do that?" Paul asked.

"It won't be easy, Mr. Barclay," Markum replied seriously. "But I think I know what to do."

CHAPTER 5

Jake Suggs

Jake Suggs read the morning paper with great interest. Most people in town knew Jake as a handyman. But if anyone were to ask him his profession, he'd say, "Professional hunting guide." During the fall of each year that's all he did.

As soon as bear season opened, Jake left his tools behind and guided bear hunters. Thanks in part to his well-trained dogs, Jake's clients were usually successful. Then deer season came along in November. For Jake, that meant six more weeks of guiding hunters.

A native of the area, Jake had hunted around Bear Lake for over 15 years. As a result he knew those woods as well as anyone in the entire state. *It would be a real feather in my cap*, Jake thought, *if I could nail whatever it is that's attacking people up there.* The more he thought about it, the more the idea appealed to him.

Two days later Jake loaded up his ATV. He took food, his 30/06 deer rifle, 20 rounds of ammunition, and his tent and sleeping bag. Cages for Millie and Buck, his two dogs, went in the small trailer he'd be towing. He wrapped two frozen hind quarters of venison and strapped them on top of the dog cages. *This will make great bait for whatever it is that I'm after*, he thought.

Just before driving off, Jake called his friend, Nick Collins. "Hi, Nick. It's Jake. Listen, buddy, I need a favor."

"Sure, Jake. What is it?"

"I'm going to Bear Lake to hunt down the 'mystery beast' that's been in the news," Jake replied. "Would you be willing to run up there in a couple of days? By then I'll need fresh supplies of food, ice— stuff like that."

"No problem, Jake," Nick responded.

"Thanks a lot, Nick. I'll be set up near the old Boy Scout campsite. Do you know the spot?"

"Yeah," Nick replied. "I know it."

"Great," Jake said. "If I'm out hunting, just leave the stuff by my tent."

"Okay, buddy," Nick said, "and good luck with your hunt."

It was 3:00 P.M. when Jake arrived at the shore of Bear Lake. Sensing an upcoming hunt, Mollie and Buck ran around excitedly. After pitching his tent, Jake got a good fire going. Then he broke out some food for himself and the dogs.

Jake also loaded five rounds of ammunition into his rifle and placed it next to his tent. He counted on the dogs to warn him if anything came near.

Just before sunset, Jake walked 300 yards down the shore. Around the trunk of a large oak tree he tied one of the venison hindquarters. Then, after tethering Mollie and Buck to a big tree near his tent, he crawled into his sleeping bag.

The next morning, Jake walked down to the lake to check his bait. To his amazement the entire hunk of venison was gone! It had been carried away so quietly that neither of the dogs had barked.

Whatever it is I'm hunting, Jake thought, *has to be very smart and resourceful. I guess I'd better change my approach.*

Jake searched the woods all day, but found nothing. So that evening he tied the second hindquarter to the same tree. But instead of returning to his tent, Jake rigged a small blind just 80 yards away. He was determined to spend the night there, watching the bait in the moonlight.

After caging the dogs, he returned to the blind and settled in for the night. Jake Suggs never saw the morning sun rise. Sometime in the middle of the night, he was attacked from behind by the animal he was hunting. The hunter had become the hunted.

Two days later Nick Collins arrived at

Bear Lake with Jake's provisions. Right away he sensed that something was wrong. For one thing, Mollie and Buck were caged. If Jake was hunting, the dogs would be with him. Nick opened the cages and the animals bounded down the shore. Nick was in hot pursuit. About 300 yards away, Nick spotted Jake's rifle and hat on the ground. He gasped when he saw what was left of Jake's blind. Something had hit it with tremendous force. Bits and pieces were scattered over a 10-yard area. And there was blood everywhere—lots of it.

Nick's trip down the mountain was very sad. From what he'd seen, there was little doubt that his friend was dead. Since he couldn't drive both ATVs, he took Jake's with the trailer and the dogs. The next day he'd come back to pick up his own vehicle and the supplies.

The minute Nick hit town, he went to the police station to report the attack.

The Plan

Professor Markum was giving a crash course on tigers to Roy Bell, Tim Ward, and Paul Barclay. "Tigers have a keen sense of smell, excellent eyesight, and exceptional hearing. Do you know why they're called the 'ultimate predators'?" Markum asked. "Because their prey never sees them until they're ready to strike. They won't attack until they're close enough for a quick kill. When they're ready, they'll strike—almost always from behind."

Tim Ward had a question. "Professor, is it true that hunters in India sometimes wear masks? I've heard they wear them on the back of their heads to confuse tigers."

"Yes, that's true," Markum replied. "A fake face in back draws attention from the real face in front. A tiger may not know which is which. Some people believe this confusion deters attacks."

Paul wasn't much interested in tiger trivia. "Why haven't we found any of the victims?" he asked bluntly.

"Many predators eat their prey where it drops," the professor went on. "Tigers, however, carry their kill deep in their territory. And a tiger can *carry*, not drag, its kill. That explains why no one's been able to find a trail."

"Do you think we can capture this tiger?" Chief Bell asked.

"Yes, Chief, I do," Markum replied. "We know that it prowls the shoreline of Bear Lake. I think we should place a large cage up there. If we bait it with fresh meat, it's just a matter of time. Fresh meat is important because tigers aren't scavengers. They're not interested in rotting or decaying food."

Ward scratched his head. "Do you know where we can get a cage large enough to do the job?" he asked.

"I do indeed!" Markum exclaimed. "And I've taken the liberty of arranging for it to be flown in. The cage will arrive at the airport tomorrow. Has the area been closed to the public, Chief?"

"Yes, it has," the Chief confirmed. "My men have put up NO TRESPASSING signs all around Bear Lake."

"Good," Markum said. "Now there's just one last thing I must mention."

"What's that?" the other three men asked in unison.

Markum caught the eyes of each man for a moment. "We'll need a couple of people on the site to keep an eye on the cage," he said.

Markum paused to check out each man's reaction. When they continued to hold his gaze without blinking, he continued with his plan. "All the attacks so far have been near the shoreline. So I think the safest observation point would be out on the lake. A 20- to 22-foot boat with a small cutty cabin would be perfect. We could anchor it about 50 yards offshore. The observers would be quite comfortable—but most importantly, they'd be safe from attack."

"The boat is no problem," Paul said. "I have one that's perfect for the job."

"Wonderful!" the professor exclaimed. "After the helicopter drops off the cage, it can go back and pick up your boat. With any luck at all we can capture our tiger in a day or two."

At the airport Paul Barclay studied the 8-by-14–foot tiger cage. It was made out of a light, but very strong, wire mesh. At the back was a large hook for hanging the bait. A cable ran from the hook to a pin that held the front door open. When an animal disturbed the bait, the pin would pull and the door would slam shut. *Very clever,* Paul thought to himself.

It was late afternoon before the cage was baited and in place. Paul's boat was now anchored about 40 yards offshore.

Professor Markum and Tim Ward had agreed to take the first watch. They were about to row the small dinghy out to Paul's boat. "We'll be back to relieve you at this time tomorrow," Paul said. Then he and the Chief hopped in the helicopter.

As night wore on, a heavy cloud cover began to roll in over the lake. The weak moonlight quickly disappeared. Tim was sleeping in the cabin. Alone in the stern of the boat, Professor Markum peered into the darkness. *I may as well get some sleep, too,* he thought. *Under this cloud cover I can't see a darn thing!*

Then suddenly, a loud metallic bang echoed through the night. Professor Markum jumped up and gasped. *That can only be one thing,* he thought. *We've caught something in our cage!*

Close Call

The professor was as excited as a five-year-old opening birthday gifts. He woke Tim Ward and exclaimed, "We've got our creature in the cage, Tim!"

Tim leaped up. "How do you know? Can you see what it is?" he asked.

"No, it's much too d-dark," Markum said, his voice catching from excitement. "But judging from the banging sounds, the cat is big—and it's none too happy."

Tim looked at his watch. It was 3:00 A.M. "So we'll wait until daylight," he said. "I'll make us a pot of coffee."

"No, no, Tim! Let's row ashore *now*," Markum urged. "I can't wait to get a look at that tiger."

"No way! We're not going to do that, Professor," Tim cautioned. "There are other large animals in these woods besides your tiger. If something else is in the cage, your tiger is still on the loose. And if *that's* the case, you don't want to be walking the shoreline in the middle of the night."

"I guess you're right," Markum replied.

Gradually, darkness gave way to dawn. As they reached the cage, neither man could believe his eyes. A large black bear was inside! "How are we going to get him out of there?" the professor asked.

"Very carefully," Ward replied.

The two men were very disappointed. For the past three hours they'd been hopeful that they'd caught the large cat. Not knowing what else to do, Tim got on the cell phone and called Roy Bell. "Good morning, Chief, I hope I didn't wake you."

"No problem, Tim," the Chief said. "I've been up for an hour. Did you catch anything last night?"

"Yes, Chief," Tim said with a sigh, "but not what we were after. It's a big black bear. We need a ladder to get on top of the cage. That's the only way we can safely open the door to let him out."

"Okay, Tim," the Chief replied. "I'll have Paul bring one up when he comes. He and his son are going to relieve you about noon. I'd planned to join him, but other issues are demanding my attention. Don't worry, Tim. Paul and his son can handle the next shift."

At midday Paul and Aaron arrived on the scene in an ATV. Tied on top was a 12-foot extension ladder. After Tim and the Professor rowed ashore, the team members discussed their next move.

It was agreed that Tim and Markum would open the door to release the bear. They'd be out of harm's way on top of the cage. And the Barclays would also be safe as they waited in the dinghy on the lake.

The operation went smoothly. Once

the cage door opened, the bear bolted for the woods, never looking back. After resetting the trap for another try, Tim and Markum drove down the mountain in the ATV. Paul and Aaron rowed out to the boat to begin their watch.

Just as darkness was falling, Aaron spoke to his father. "You know, Dad, my sister is a pretty special person."

Paul's eyes widened in surprise. "Gee, son," he said. "*I* know that—but I wasn't sure that *you* did. What happened to make you realize it?"

Aaron looked thoughtful. "Well, I was just thinking," he replied. "We're safe on this boat in the middle of the lake. But when Pam heard her friend scream, she charged right into danger. The tiger could have attacked her, too."

"You're right, son," Paul agreed. "She *is* a brave girl. Do you remember the time she pulled you out of the well?"

"Do I ever! How could I forget?" Aaron

exclaimed. "She reminds me of it at least three times a week!"

Paul chuckled. He was about to say something more when he noticed some movement on the shore. As he peered through his binoculars he groaned, "Oh, no."

"What is it, Dad?" Aaron asked.

"It's a red fox, son," Paul replied. "I think he smelled our bait. Gosh, I sure hope he doesn't release the cage door."

Aaron looked surprised. "Isn't a fox too small to do that?" he asked.

Paul looked troubled. "I'm not sure, son," he said. "That pin is pretty sensitive. I don't think it would take much pressure to release it."

A moment later they had their answer. Tugging on the hanging meat, the little fox pulled the pin and was trapped inside. Paul looked at Aaron and shrugged. "I'm sorry, Aaron, but we have to get him out of there. We need to reset the trap now. If we don't, this whole night will be a loss."

After rowing ashore, Paul told Aaron to stay in the dinghy as he approached the cage. Then he opened the door and reset the pin. As quick as a wink the little fox scampered back into the woods.

About 40 yards away, just on the edge of the woods, a pair of keen eyes was watching. Then, suddenly, 350 pounds of raw fury bounded from the brush and headed straight for Paul.

Aaron could see the big cat in the moonlight. "It's the tiger, Dad! RUN!"

Paul immediately realized that he couldn't reach the dinghy in time. His only hope was to get into the water.

While watching his father's race with death, Aaron paddled the dinghy out into deep water. The tiger was just five yards behind Paul as he dove in and swam underwater. The big cat looked very disappointed when Paul surfaced 25 yards from shore.

Trembling in exhaustion, Paul scrambled up the boat ladder. For a few moments he sat hunched over, dripping wet and gasping for air.

Aaron was fighting back tears. "The tiger leaped right after you dove, Dad! With all the splashing and the dim light, I wasn't sure what had happened. For a minute I thought the tiger had caught you for sure."

Paul smiled and put his arm around his son. "That was a close call, all right!" he said, still gasping. "I haven't run that fast since my days on the college track team!"

Success at Last

"Do you think the tiger will come back tonight?" Aaron asked nervously.

"I think there's a good chance, Aaron," Paul replied. "We know that he's hungry, or he wouldn't have charged me like that. And out here on the lake, we present no threat to him. Yeah, I think there's an excellent chance that he'll be back."

"All that excitement has made *me* hungry, too," Aaron answered. "Could you eat a ham sandwich if I made you one?"

Paul smiled at his son's offer. "Sure, son. Put mustard on mine, okay?"

For a few minutes they sat in the boat, eating and talking quietly. It was almost midnight when Aaron said, "I think I'll grab a few hours of sleep now—if that's all right with you, Dad."

Paul patted Aaron on the back. "Good idea, son," he said. "Get some rest. I'll wake you if anything happens."

Aaron paused at the door to the cabin. "You won't take the dinghy and go ashore alone, will you, Dad?"

"No, Aaron," Paul promised. "One close call with that creature is enough to last me for a while!"

Three hours later Paul was staring at the stars. His mind was miles and miles from Bear Lake. Then the quiet of the night was interrupted by a slamming sound. A menacing, deep-throated growl followed the abrupt clanging of the cage door.

Paul grabbed his binoculars. In the pale moonlight he could make out the body of a large cat. It was locked in the cage! At first he was struck by the size of the animal. The professor must have underestimated its weight. It had to be eight or even nine feet long! Its large, square head jutted out from massive shoulders. Powerful muscles rippled throughout its body as it paced back and forth. The thought that this animal had almost caught him sent cold shivers down Paul's spine.

Paul also marveled at the sheer beauty of the beast. In addition to its size and strength, the tiger was truly a spectacular sight. Its smooth, silky-looking coat seemed to be a tawny color—somewhere between tan and gold. And its distinctive black stripes were unmistakable—the universal markings of a tiger.

But what *really* held Paul's attention were its eyes. As Paul studied them through the binoculars, the tiger's dark, piercing stare made him shudder. This marvelous animal was truly the king of its domain—and he knew it!

After telling Aaron the good news, Paul called Roy Bell on the cell phone. "Sorry to wake you in the middle of the night, Roy. But I thought you'd want to know that we got him!"

"That's great news, Paul!" the Chief exclaimed. "I'll let Markum know right away. He can arrange for a 'copter flight first thing tomorrow. I'll drive the ATV and plan to arrive at the same time."

The next morning Paul could hear the engine's roar before he could see the helicopter. Minutes later it appeared over the treetops. As it landed on the lakeshore, Chief Bell arrived on the ATV.

"Well, Professor," Paul said, "It looks like you got your wish."

Professor Markum didn't respond. He couldn't take his eyes off of the cage and the large animal pacing inside. "Look at him, gentlemen! Isn't he magnificent?"

"No one would argue with that," Roy Bell replied. "But let's also remember how deadly he is. He's already killed a minimum of three people."

"I know that, Chief," Markum replied. "And believe me, my heart goes out to the families of the unfortunate victims. But it wasn't my fault that the tiger escaped."

"Don't worry, Professor," Chief Bell assured him. "No one is blaming *you* for the deaths! But it would be smart to get your creation out of this area ASAP. Think about it: People who've lost a family member may not think that beast is as magnificent as you do."

The professor nodded. "I couldn't agree with you more. In fact, an excellent facility has already agreed to take the 'liger.' Did I tell you that's what we're calling this cross between a lion and a tiger? A new two-acre enclosure is being prepared at the San Diego Zoo. I'm told it will be ready within a couple of days."

The helicopter pilot had been standing by, listening to their conversation. Now he spoke up impatiently: "Hey, guys, I only get paid to *fly* this bird. Can we cut the gabbing and get the heck out of here?"

Chief Bell glanced at Paul. "The man's got a point," Paul said with a grin.

Markum and Bell climbed aboard the helicopter. Moments later the aircraft lifted about 10 feet off the ground. Paul and Aaron hooked up the cage to the hovering helicopter. Then they stepped back, and Paul flashed the pilot an "all clear" signal.

Standing on the shore of the lake, father and son watched the 'copter until it was out of sight. It was time to go home. After loading their gear onto the ATV, they headed down the trail.

Back to Square One

The flight from Bear Lake to the airport should have been a quick one. Normally, it would take about 25 minutes to get there. But this trip would be different.

In his haste to get under way, the pilot had made a serious miscalculation: He'd misjudged the weight load. He'd figured on three full-grown men and the cage dangling 25 feet below. But the 'copter was also carrying a 350-pound animal. This additional burden was just slightly more than the aircraft could handle safely.

About five minutes after takeoff, the helicopter was skimming the treetops on the mountainside. Then the cage got snagged in the top of a tall pine tree.

Jerked by the snagged cable, the 'copter nosedived toward the forest floor.

The pilot frantically tried to correct the situation. But it was too late to avoid a crash landing. He cut the engine—but the rotor blades had snapped in the treetops! Luckily, the helicopter came to a stop about 10 feet off the ground in a thick canopy of trees.

Quickly shaking the cobwebs from his brain, Roy Bell said, "Is everybody okay?"

The first person to answer was Professor Markum. "I think I am," he said. Next the pilot spoke up. "I'm okay, too, but this machine has had it. I think we're going to have to walk out of here."

Markum suddenly thought about the valuable cargo they were carrying. "Oh, no! Where's the cage?" he cried out to no one in particular.

The pilot reached under his seat and grabbed a long piece of rope. He tied one end to a strut under the instrument panel and kicked open his side door. When all three men had slid down safely, they looked back in shock.

The cage was lying on its side. But there was a gaping five-foot hole in it. It was empty! The liger was gone!

For a moment, not a word was spoken. Each man was lost in his own thoughts. Professor Markum was devastated by the loss of his prized creation. Chief Bell was horrified at the thought of a killer animal on the loose again. And, realizing the crash was his fault, the pilot was worried about his job.

They had no choice but to start the long trek back toward town. "Let's get a move on," Chief Bell said. "I don't want to be stuck out here after dark."

* * * *

When they reached town, Paul and Aaron had headed directly for the airport. Neither one of them wanted to miss the look on people's faces as they saw their first liger. As they pulled up to the terminal, they were surprised at how quiet it was. *Where were all the people?* Rushing into the office, Paul asked, "Where's the 'copter that went up to Bear Lake?"

He was told it hadn't returned yet.

A worried look came over Paul's face. "It hasn't arrived?" he said. "But they left the lake more than two hours ago. They should have been here by now."

News of the overdue helicopter soon had everyone scrambling. Another 'copter was sent up to investigate. Minutes later the pilot radioed back that a crash site had been found—but there was no sign of survivors. Meanwhile, Roy and the others could hear the second 'copter passing over as they trudged along. But the forest was too thick and dense for either party to see the other.

"Well, at least we know they're out looking for us," the pilot said.

"Yeah," Roy grumbled. "But they'll never see us in all this brush. We have to get closer to the main road."

It was nearly noon when the trio

stumbled out of the forest. Soon after they found a paved road, a patrol car picked them up. "Am I glad to see you, Chief!" the officer exlaimed. "The whole department has been worried sick."

"Thanks," Chief Bell answered. "I'm glad we didn't take down all those NO TRESPASSING signs. With that beast on the loose again, it looks like we'll be starting from scratch."

"Yes, Chief. But now we have one more problem, I'm sorry to say," Professor Markum said with a sigh.

"What's that?" the Chief asked.

"Having been caught once, the liger will be on his guard from now on. Catching him a second time is going to be a lot more difficult. Remember what I told you? Tigers are *very* intelligent animals."

What Does It Mean?

Two months had passed. The escaped liger had not been caught despite the best efforts of several agencies. But workers from the state's Forestry and the Fish and Game Departments were still on the job.

New cages had been built and placed in half a dozen locations around Bear Lake. Forestry staff checked them daily. They also changed the bait on a regular basis so the meat was always fresh. During that two-month period, several wild animals had tripped the cage doors and then been released. But there was still no sign of the liger.

Everyone was discouraged. There was even some talk of abandoning the project.

After all, it was expensive to send people up to Bear Lake to check the traps and change the bait. And none of the departments had money to waste. Besides, officials said, the creature hadn't been seen since the helicopter crash. And there had been no additional attacks on humans.

Some people believed that Professor Markum's creation was dead. Perhaps it had been seriously injured in the crash. It may have crawled out of the damaged cage and died somewhere in the thick forest. At first Roy Bell and Tim Ward didn't believe that. But as the weeks dragged on, they had to admit that it was a possibility.

The Higgins Institute had assigned Professor Markum to a project in another state. When he left, Roy promised to keep him up to date on their progress. But so far he had nothing to report.

Now another problem was looming. The Chief was worrying about the opening of hunting season—just a few weeks away. Every fall, hundreds of deer hunters were attracted to the thousands of wooded acres around Bear Lake. And hunters weren't the only eager visitors. Hikers and nature lovers were also putting pressure on the police to open the woods.

Finally, Chief Bell called a meeting of all departments involved in the recapture attempt. The meeting lasted less than an hour. All agreed to call off the search and reopen the woods. The authorities now concluded that the liger had probably died from injuries suffered in the helicopter crash.

After the meeting Tim Ward turned to Roy. "If that thing is still alive," he said, "we should know it within the next five to six weeks."

"What makes you say that, Tim?" the Chief asked.

"Next month there'll be hundreds of hunters tramping through those woods. If there's a beast to be found there, at least one of them will come across it."

Chief Bell nodded his head in

agreement. "You may be right, Tim," he said. "I hope we don't find out the hard way."

* * * *

Roy Bell breathed a sigh of relief when the hunting season passed without incident. The prospect of more deaths had made him very uneasy. By now it had been almost five months since they'd walked away from the crashed helicopter. *The beast must be dead*, he thought.

As winter came on, Roy Bell finally pushed the previous summer's ordeal to the back of his mind. After all, as Chief of Police, he had plenty of other things to occupy his mind. Of course Rockdale wasn't exactly a hotbed of major crime. But some crimes *were* committed there. There was plenty of work to keep the Chief and his officers busy.

Then one day in early February the desk sergeant took a call. After a brief conversation, the sergeant hurried over to Chief Bell's office. "Chief, I think you may want to talk to this caller yourself."

Roy picked up the phone and said, "Chief Bell here."

"Hello, Chief," said a friendly male voice. "I was just telling the other officer what happened. Some friends and I were cross-country skiing yesterday up near Bear Lake. We came across the half-eaten carcass of a dead deer."

"Well, that's not really unusual," Roy answered. "Predators take quite a few deer every winter."

"Oh, I know that, Chief," the man quickly replied. "That wasn't what was so interesting. The really mysterious thing about this kill was the tracks we saw in the snow. They appear to have been made by a very large *cat*!"

COMPREHENSION QUESTIONS

Remembering Details

1. Tim Ward was the head of what state agency?

2. What one item belonging to "Red" Wilson did the search party find?

3. What did Pam use to bind her friend's injured arm?

4. What kind of animal was the first to get caught in Professor Markum's cage?

5. What does the acronym *ATV* stand for?

6. What two details did Pam remember about the creature that followed them through the woods?

7. What name did Professor Markum give to the hybrid of a tiger and a mountain lion?

Who and Where?

1. Who liked to describe himself as a "professional hunting guide"?

2. Where did Professor Markum work as a research biologist?

3. Who was Pam Barclay's running partner?

4. Who was Rockdale's Chief of Police?

5. What part of Sam Cutts's body did the search party recover?

6. What well-known animal facility had agreed to house Professor Markum's "creation"?